SHADOW THE BRAVE DOBERMAN: A TAIL-WAGGING ADVENTURE

BELONGS TO

....

This is a work of fiction. Names, characters, businesses,
organizations, places, events, and incidents either are the
product of the author's imagination or are used fictitiously. Any
resemblance to actual persons, living or dead, events, or locales is
entirely coincidental.

The following trademarked terms are mentioned in this book:
Emma Afia. The use of these trademarks does not
indicate an endorsement of this work by the trademark owners.
The trademarks are used in a purely descriptive sense and all
trademark rights remain with the trademark owner.

Cover design by el Emma afia.

This book was typeset in Emma afia.

First edition, 2023.

Published by Emma Afia.

Chapter 1: A Mysterious Arrival

- Introduce Shadow, the brave Doberman, as the protagonist.
- Shadow mysteriously appears at the doorstep of a kind-hearted family.
- The family, intrigued by his arrival, decides to adopt him.
- Shadow's journey in his new home begins.

Chapter 2: City Sights and Sounds

- Shadow explores the bustling city streets with his new family.
- He encounters various sights, like tall buildings, noisy traffic, and crowded parks.
- Shadow makes new friends, including a mischievous squirrel and a friendly neighborhood cat.
- Together, they navigate the city's challenges and enjoy playful adventures.

Chapter 3: Into the Enchanted Forest

- Shadow and his family embark on a weekend trip to a nearby enchanted forest.
- In the forest, they meet a wise old owl who tells them about a hidden treasure.
- Shadow, filled with curiosity, takes it upon himself to find the treasure and bring back its magic.
- Along the way, he encounters magical creatures and overcomes obstacles with his bravery.

Chapter 4: Unmasking the Mystery

- Shadow's quest for the treasure leads him to a series of riddles and clues.
- With his family's support, he deciphers the puzzles, revealing the secret of the treasure.
- The treasure turns out to be an ancient artifact that holds the power to heal and unite.
- Shadow learns the importance of selflessness and the true meaning of the treasure.

Chapter 5: A Hero's Return

- Armed with the knowledge and power of the treasure, Shadow returns home.
- He uses the treasure's magic to bring joy and healing to his family and community.
- The city celebrates Shadow as a hero, recognizing his courage and selflessness.
- Shadow's journey comes full circle as he realizes that the greatest treasure of all is the love and friendship he shares with his family and friends.

Chapter 1

A Mysterious Arrival

Shadow, the brave Doberman, appeared at the doorstep of the Johnson family on a moonlit night. His sleek black coat shimmered under the glow of the streetlights, and his amber eyes held an air of mystery. The Johnsons, amazed by the sudden appearance of the gentle yet enigmatic dog, decided to take him in as their own.

As Shadow settled into his new home, he showcased his loyalty and affection for his new family. Mrs. Johnson, a kind-hearted woman, quickly formed a strong bond with him, and the children, Sarah and Ethan, were thrilled to have a new furry friend to play with.

However, questions lingered in everyone's minds. Where did Shadow come from? How did he end up on their doorstep? The family speculated about his past, but the answers remained elusive.

In the following days, Shadow explored the neighborhood, sniffing out every corner, and making new acquaintances. He won the hearts of the neighbors with his gentle nature and wagging tail. Mr. Jenkins, an elderly man living next door, grew fond of Shadow and often shared stories of his own dog from years past.

As the days went by, Shadow's mysterious arrival became a topic of conversation in the community. Rumors swirled, ranging from tales of a wandering adventurer to a legendary dog with magical powers. The truth remained uncertain, but one thing was clear: Shadow had brought an undeniable spark of joy and curiosity to the Johnson family and the neighborhood.

Little did they know that Shadow's presence would soon lead them on a remarkable journey filled with adventure, friendship, and discovery. With every passing day, the bond between Shadow and the Johnsons grew stronger, paving the way for the exciting chapters that awaited them in their shared future.

Chapter 2

City Sights and Sounds

Shadow reveled in the vibrant energy of the city as he embarked on a journey through its bustling streets alongside the Johnson family. Towering skyscrapers loomed above, casting long shadows on the pavement below. The air buzzed with the sounds of car horns, laughter, and the chatter of busy pedestrians.

With his keen senses, Shadow absorbed every detail of the cityscape. He marveled at the colorful storefronts, where enticing smells wafted out from bakeries and restaurants. The Johnsons, too, were captivated by the city's charm, but it was Shadow who led them on unexpected adventures through its winding alleys and bustling parks.

One day, while exploring a lively park, Shadow encountered a mischievous squirrel named Nutmeg. The small creature darted from tree to tree, challenging Shadow to a game of chase. Shadow eagerly joined in, his sleek legs propelling him with agility. The park echoed with their joyful barks and laughter as they weaved through the trees, their game drawing the attention of onlookers who couldn't help but smile.

In their city explorations, Shadow and the Johnsons discovered a neighborhood cat named Whiskers. Whiskers was known for her wise demeanor and a hint of mystery in her eyes. Shadow approached her with caution, unsure of her intentions. To his surprise, Whiskers extended a paw of friendship, recognizing Shadow's kind heart. They soon became unlikely companions, embarking on playful escapades through the hidden nooks and crannies of the city.

Shadow's adventures in the city introduced him to a multitude of sights, sounds, and scents. He encountered street performers who mesmerized passersby with their talents, from musicians to jugglers. He discovered hidden parks and tranquil gardens, providing a respite from the bustling streets. Shadow's natural curiosity and fearlessness allowed him to embrace every new experience, forging unforgettable memories for the Johnson family and himself.

Through their city explorations, Shadow, Nutmeg, Whiskers, and the Johnsons formed a tight-knit bond. They learned that friendship can be found in unexpected places and that the city, with all its excitement and challenges, was a vast playground waiting to be explored. As the chapter came to a close, Shadow and his newfound companions eagerly anticipated the adventures that awaited them beyond the city's borders, ready to embark on the next leg of their remarkable journey.

Chapter 3

Into the Enchanted Forest

The Johnson family decided it was time for a weekend getaway, seeking a change of scenery from the bustling city. Their destination was an enchanting forest rumored to be a place of magic and wonder. With Shadow leading the way, they set off on an adventure into the unknown.

As they entered the forest, the air grew cooler, and the sunlight filtered through the tall trees, creating dappled patterns on the forest floor. Shadow's senses heightened as he breathed in the earthy scent of moss and listened to the rustling leaves overhead.

In their wanderings, they stumbled upon a majestic old oak tree where a wise owl named Hootie perched. Hootie's eyes gleamed with ancient wisdom as he shared tales of the forest's secrets. He revealed that deep within the heart of the forest lay a hidden treasure, said to possess extraordinary powers of healing and unity.

Intrigued by the prospect of such a treasure, Shadow's curiosity soared. Determined to uncover its whereabouts, he led the Johnsons further into the dense foliage, encountering magical creatures along the way. They met playful fairies flitting among the flowers, mischievous sprites hiding in the shadows, and gentle woodland creatures who shared their wisdom.

As the sun began to set, casting a warm glow through the forest, Shadow and his family stumbled upon a series of riddles and clues left by the forest's magical inhabitants. Together, they deciphered the cryptic messages, each clue leading them closer to the hidden treasure. Along their journey, they encountered challenges that tested their resolve. They navigated treacherous paths, crossed babbling brooks on rickety bridges, and faced their deepest fears. Through it all, Shadow's bravery and unwavering determination shone, inspiring his family to push forward.

Finally, after overcoming the final obstacle, they reached a hidden glen bathed in soft moonlight. Before them stood a stone pedestal, upon which rested the fabled treasure—a shimmering gem radiating with an otherworldly glow.

As they approached, the gem revealed its secret. It wasn't merely a material treasure but a source of love, compassion, and harmony. Shadow realized that the true power of the treasure lay in how it could bring people together, heal wounds, and bridge divides.

Filled with a newfound understanding, Shadow and the Johnsons returned from the enchanted forest, carrying the treasure's magic within them. They understood that true treasures lay not in material possessions, but in the bonds they forged and the love they shared.

With hearts filled with gratitude and a deeper appreciation for the world around them, they looked forward to spreading the treasure's magic beyond the forest, bringing joy and unity to all those they encountered. Their adventure in the enchanted forest had transformed them, setting the stage for the next chapter of their extraordinary journey.

Chapter 4

Unmasking the Mystery

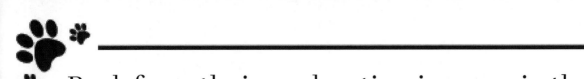

Back from their enchanting journey in the forest, Shadow and the Johnson family found themselves in a contemplative state. The treasure they had discovered had touched their hearts and opened their minds to the true power of love and unity. However, they couldn't help but wonder about the origins and purpose of the mystical gem.

Driven by their curiosity, they delved deeper into the mystery surrounding the treasure. They searched through old books, consulted wise sages, and sought out ancient legends. Eventually, their efforts bore fruit, and they stumbled upon a forgotten tale passed down through generations. The legend spoke of a time long ago when the world was fractured, divided by conflicts and misunderstandings. It told of a great guardian, a dog with a heart of gold, who possessed the ability to heal and bring people together. This guardian, it seemed, was none other than Shadow himself.

Armed with this newfound knowledge, Shadow and the Johnsons realized that the treasure they had discovered was a symbol—a reminder of the guardian's mission to spread love, harmony, and understanding. They felt a sense of purpose and a responsibility to share the gem's magic with the world.

They embarked on a journey to spread the treasure's power of healing and unity. Shadow and the Johnsons visited schools, community centers, and hospitals, sharing stories of their adventures and the lessons they had learned. They encouraged empathy, compassion, and embracing diversity.

As they traveled from place to place, they witnessed the transformative impact of the treasure's magic. Hearts were touched, friendships were forged, and people were inspired to make positive changes in their own lives and communities.

The news of Shadow's mission spread far and wide. Soon, others joined them in their quest, forming a network of individuals dedicated to creating a more harmonious world. They became an unstoppable force of love and unity, working together to mend the fractures that had divided society.

Shadow's journey had evolved from a personal adventure to a mission of global significance. The Johnsons, filled with pride, watched as their loyal companion became a symbol of hope, demonstrating the power of love and compassion to transcend barriers.

As they continued their quest, Shadow and the Johnsons knew that their work was far from over. There were still hearts to heal, bridges to build, and lives to touch. With unwavering determination, they pressed on, ready to face whatever challenges lay ahead, knowing that the treasure's magic would guide and empower them.

The chapter closed with a sense of anticipation, as Shadow and his dedicated allies prepared to extend their reach further, their bond and purpose stronger than ever. They were determined to make a difference in the world, one act of kindness at a time, ready for the remarkable adventures that awaited them in the next chapter of their extraordinary journey.

Chapter 5

A Hero's Return

After their tireless efforts to spread the treasure's magic of love and unity, Shadow and the Johnson family found themselves on the cusp of a remarkable homecoming. The city where their journey began eagerly awaited their return, ready to celebrate their accomplishments and honor their unwavering dedication.

As they made their way back, whispers of their heroic deeds filled the air. The news of Shadow's transformative impact had reached far and wide, inspiring individuals from all walks of life. The city's residents, filled with gratitude and admiration, prepared a grand celebration to honor Shadow and his companions.

The day of their arrival arrived, and the city's main square bustled with excitement. Banners fluttered in the breeze, adorned with images of Shadow, his noble silhouette a symbol of hope and unity. The square was packed with people, young and old, eagerly awaiting their beloved hero's return.

As Shadow and the Johnson family stepped onto the stage, a wave of applause and cheers erupted. The crowd's gratitude was palpable, their love for Shadow evident in every smile and teary eye. The mayor of the city stepped forward, acknowledging the immense impact of Shadow's journey and the treasure's magic on the community.

In a heartfelt speech, the mayor praised Shadow and the Johnsons for their selflessness, courage, and unwavering commitment to making the world a better place. She declared that from that day forward, Shadow would be known as the honorary Guardian of Unity, recognized for his exceptional ability to bridge divides and inspire compassion. With tears of joy streaming down their faces, the Johnson family accepted the honorary title on behalf of Shadow. They expressed their gratitude to the city and its residents for their unwavering support and shared how their own lives had been transformed by the remarkable journey they had undertaken together.

The celebration continued with music, dance, and laughter reverberating through the streets. Shadow, surrounded by friends and well-wishers, wagged his tail with delight, knowing that his mission of love and unity had touched countless lives.

In the months that followed, Shadow and the Johnsons continued their tireless efforts to spread the treasure's magic, not just within their city but far beyond. They became ambassadors of compassion, traveling to distant lands, helping communities in need, and inspiring others to believe in the power of unity.

As time passed, Shadow's legend grew, his story inspiring generations to come. The treasure's magic became a timeless symbol of hope, reminding people that even in the face of adversity, love and unity could prevail.

And so, the chapter came to a close, with Shadow and the Johnsons embracing their roles as guardians of compassion and continuing their mission to heal hearts, mend fractures, and build bridges. They knew that their journey would never truly end, for the work of love and unity was a lifelong commitment.

With heads held high and hearts filled with purpose, they set off into the sunset, ready to face new challenges and spread the treasure's magic wherever it was needed most. Shadow, the honorary Guardian of Unity, embarked on the next phase of his extraordinary journey, knowing that together with his dedicated allies, they could create a brighter, more harmonious world—one act of kindness at a time.

The End

This is a work of fiction. Names, characters, businesses, organizations, places, events, and incidents either are the product of the author's imagination or are used fictitiously. Any resemblance to actual persons, living or dead, events, or locales is entirely coincidental.

Cover design by el Emma afia.

This book was typeset in Emma afia.

First edition, 2023.

Published by Emma Afia.

12092556R00018